GLADIATOR BOY

vs

THE THREE NINJAS

GLADIATOR BOY

Win an exclusive
Gladiator Boy T-shirt and goody bag!

Use the special code below to decode the sentence, then send it in to us.
Each month we will draw one winner to receive a Gladiator Boy T-shirt
and goody bag.

Send your entry on a postcard to:
GLADIATOR BOY: ESCAPE FROM THE EAST COMPETITION,
Hodder Children's Books, 338 Euston Road, London NW1 3BH

Only one entry per child.
Final Draw: 31 December 2010

You can also enter this competition via the Gladiator Boy website

WWW.GLADIATORBOY.COM

GLADIATOR BOY vs

THE THREE NINJAS

DAVID GRIMSTONE

Hodder
Children's
Books

A division of Hachette Children's Books

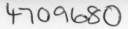

For Matthew Doy, for many years of good friendship.

This new series is dedicated to Leilani Sparrow, who has worked tirelessly with Gladiator Boy since his arrival. Thanks also to Anne McNeil, who has stood in my corner since day one.

HOW MANY

GLADIATOR BOY

BOOKS DO YOU HAVE?

DAVID GRIMSTONE

GLADIATOR BOY

A HERO'S QUEST

DAVID GRIMSTONE

GLADIATOR BOY

STOWAWAY SLAVES

FREE GLADIATOR GAME INSIDE

DAVID GRIMSTONE

GLADIATOR BOY

ESCAPE FROM EVIL

FREE GLADIATOR GAME INSIDE

GLADIATOR BOY

THE REBELS' ASSAULT

DAVID GRIMSTONE

GLADIATOR BOY

RESCUE MISSION

FREE GLADIATOR GAME INSIDE

DAVID GRIMSTONE

GLADIATOR BOY

THE BLADE OF FIRE

FREE GLADIATOR GAME INSIDE

CHINA

PREVIOUSLY IN GLADIATOR BOY

At the request of Slavious Doom, Decimus and his friends are plunged into King D'Tong's deadly water maze. After a series of near-death incidents, Gladius manages to save the group from a watery grave by destroying a wooden prop holding up the maze. Unfortunately, things quickly go from bad to worse, and the slaves find themselves plummeting over the edge of a perilously vast waterfall . . .

CHAPTER
I

TROUBLE
AT THE
FALLS

S lavious Doom raged into the throne room of King D'Tong and kicked out at one of the great marble pillars. 'They've escaped your water maze!' he screamed. 'ALL of them, together! I thought you said that trap was fatal! You told me ... no, in fact, you promised me that those flooded tunnels were impossible to escape! Decimus Rex has completely humiliated you, just as he

did me in my arena in Italy!'

Despite the rising anger in Doom's voice, the king merely smiled and shook his head slowly. When he spoke, his own voice was calm and measured.

'Worry you not, Doom Lord,' he said. 'They will not get far.'

D'Tong sat up sharply, and clapped his wrinkled hands.

'Miriki! Aritezu! Tekaro!'

A door at the back of the throne room flew open and the three Japanese ninjas hurried in. Without a word, they formed a line at the base of the dais and bowed their heads, slightly.

'Slaves escape water maze,' he said quickly, sparing no time to explain the situation at length. 'Search waterfall. Find them. Kill all. Bring bodies here. I command it.'

The first of the three ninjas gave a curt nod, and the trio departed.

'That's it?' said Doom, doubtfully. 'A simple execution? You told me Rex and his friends would suffer unspeakable agony!'

King D'Tong released a sickly smile.

'They will,' he cackled. 'Oh . . . they will.'

Olu looked down at the strange tube that Tonino had acquired for them, and frowned. The old woman who'd sold them the device hadn't gone out of her way to explain how it worked but, even so, the tube wasn't difficult to work. You simply held it up to one eye, and tightly shut the other.

'I can see everything up close!' Olu exclaimed. 'It's amazing!'

'Yes, yes! We've established that,' said Argon, moodily. 'What can you see, exactly?'

'A waterfall.'

'Great; we need to go that way. The map shows a waterfall at the southern edge of Yelang.'

Olu still wasn't sure about the map; they'd acquired it from the same seller, the old travelling woman who'd stopped in the bay to nose around Tonino's ship. A small pot of spices generously traded on their behalf had secured the pair a strange tubular device and a map of the local area. The curious old woman had seemed to know immediately where it was they wanted to get to; a mystery in itself. Olu had suggested that this may have been because she'd already run into Decimus on her travels, and saw that he and Argon were both dressed in similar clothes.

Still, whatever the reason for her foresight, she'd done them a considerable favour.

'Should we head for the base of the falls or the top?' Argon prompted, as Olu handed him the looking-tube.

'I think we should try to get around them,

somehow. We don't want to go anywhere that narrows our view. I like to see enemies coming a long way away.'

'What about friends?' Argon grinned.

'We won't find Decimus at a waterfall,' said Olu, seriously. 'He'll have made straight for the Winter Palace . . . and so should we.'

Far, far below the rise where Olu and Argon were watching the crest of the falls, Gladius was desperately trying to find Ruma. He had already fished Decimus out of the water and dragged him on to the jagged rocks at the side of the lagoon, but of the scrawny Etrurian there was simply no sign.

He expected the worst: Decimus had been

half drowned when he'd extracted him from the water, and had needed several sharp blows on the chest before he'd spewed up the lungful of liquid inside him.

Now, with Decimus coughing and spluttering on the rocks, he dived again and again to try to find Ruma before it was too late to save him. The water beneath the surface of the lagoon was surprisingly clear, but the powerful, thundering spray of the falls caused a great bubbling wash under the waves.

At least, Gladius thought, I'm facing my fears: I've probably spent more time underwater in the last year than I ever thought I could. Hmm ... maybe danger makes you strong.

Where are you, Ruma?

Beginning to despair, Gladius took one final

dive and searched through the water beside the far bank: nothing.

Ruma was gone.

Exploding from the lagoon once again, Gladius scrambled over the rocks and crouched beside his gasping friend.

'Are you OK, Decimus?' he enquired, thumping the young gladiator in the middle of the back.

'Y-yeah.'

'Can you breathe properly yet?'

Decimus nodded. 'Did you find Ruma?'

'No . . . and certainly not for the lack of looking. I've searched every inch of this lag—'

Suddenly, and without warning, Gladius grabbed Decimus, wrenched him to his feet and hurled him back into the water. Even before the resulting splash, Gladius had leaped after him. The two friends struggled beneath the lapping tide, rolling over each other as Gladius fought to drag his friend through the water. Eventually, when they'd almost reached the base of the falls

themselves, Gladius used his strength to pull Decimus to the surface.

The young gladiator coughed out yet another jet of lagoon water.

'Are you crazy?' he exclaimed. 'I almost drowned once and you drag me back in here again? What's wrong with y—'

'Shhh!' Gladius frantically shook his friend. 'It's those three warriors who defeated us at the Winter Palace! They're coming down the path that leads through the trees! Look!'

Decimus half turned in the water, his legs kicking furiously beneath him.

'Up there!' Gladius added, pointing past him. 'If we stay here, though, and try to keep under the spray, they might not see us.'

Decimus felt a sense of desperation well up

inside him. They lost a fight against the three ninjas even when they were all fresh and full of energy; in their current state, both half-exhausted and with Ruma missing – presumed dead – they wouldn't stand a chance against them. He winced: the pain in his arm had lessened, but was still a cause for concern. Curse that water maze!

It was at this point, bobbing up and down in the lagoon beneath the spraying wash of the falls, that Decimus did something he'd rarely done before: he began to pray to the gods.

Please, lords; I know I don't worship nearly as much as your priests command, but please, don't let them see us. If we get out of this lagoon alive, I promise you all that I will worship you more often.

He opened his eyes, and immediately knew the situation had worsened.

'They're searching the banks individually,' Gladius whispered, his face fraught with worry. 'Two of them are on the opposite side of the bank, but the tallest one is heading straight for us.'

'Just keep still; there's a chance he can't see us through the spray.'

The assassin stalked up the bank towards them. When he reached the edge of the water, he crouched down and – to their horror began to squint at the spray.

'He's going to see us,' Gladius panted. 'He's looking right at me.'

Decimus knew it was true. He tensed for the inevitable shout of alarm and, sure enough, it came, loud and clear.

There were two piercing cries; it took a few seconds before Decimus realized they were not coming from the ninja who was crouched on the near bank. Instead, the call of alarm had come from one of his two companions further up the pass.

Almost immediately, the assassin heeded the cry and quickly departed.

Decimus breathed a sigh of relief.

'I was sure he'd seen us,' Gladius admitted, treading water next to him. 'It looks like they're going, though – something else must have caught their attention! Lucky for us!'

But it was unlucky for Olu and Argon.

The two friends stood in a clearing halfway

26

up the pass, and found themselves surrounded. The eerie strangers had stepped silently from the trees, and now stood in various battle stances around the clearing.

'Who are you?' Olu hazarded, staring from one black-clad figure to another. 'What do you want with us?'

He stepped back, but one of the ninjas quickly blocked his path. He made to take a similar step forward, but again the triangle of watchers shifted to cut off their exits.

'We mean you no harm,' said Argon, holding out his hands in a calming manner. 'We are strangers to this land. We merely come in search of our friends.'

There was a moment of grim silence; then all three ninjas leapt forward at once.

Olu was taken completely by surprise; the warriors moved so quickly that he barely had time to raise one arm in defence before a rain of speedy punches from one of them sent him crashing to the forest floor. The map and the looking-tube were wrenched from his grasp and tossed aside as the ninja dropped down and fixed him in a crushing headlock.

Further along the path, Argon had been

slightly more prepared. He'd seen one of the ninjas readying to pounce from the corner of his eye, and was able to catch the little warrior in mid-flight and propel him directly into a tree. However, his brief sense of victory turned to one of shock when the attacker sprang back off the trunk – having landed two-footed – and immediately catapulted himself back on to the path.

Unfortunately, Argon's attention was diverted by the manoeuvre long enough to allow the third warrior to charge bodily into his back. The Gaul flew off his feet and tumbled down the path, rolling over and over as a whirlwind of rocks and small stones were thrown up around him.

'It's Argon and Olu!' said Gladius, from the path on the opposite side of the falls. 'We have to help them!'

'We can't!' Decimus panted. 'I'm wiped out, and we wouldn't stand a chance against them anyway.'

'But they've thrown Argon down the pass!' Gladius continued. 'And it looks like they're strangling Olu! We have to do something.'

Decimus thought for a second, and then cupped two hands around his mouth.

'Over here!' he screamed. 'Ooovvvvveeeeeeer heeeeeeeeeeeeerrrrrrrreeeeee!'

Two of the ninjas turned immediately. The third tossed Olu aside like a bundle of rags, and hurried down the path to join them. In seconds, all three were dashing down the pass, leaping rocks, small bushes and various other obstacles as they went.

'Now what?' said Gladius, watching the approach with mounting trepidation.

'Now we split up,' Decimus snapped. 'You go east, I'll go west. I'll try to double back and find you once I've lost mine. Well? What are you waiting for? Didn't you hear me? You wanted to do something! So MOVE!'

The young gladiator sprinted off through the trees, screaming at the top of his voice as he fled. Gladius took a second to steady himself, then hurried away in the opposite direction, shouting as loud as his strangled breath would permit.

We don't stand a chance, he thought to himself. If they catch us, we're dead.

Two of the ninjas crossed the shallower part of the lagoon without so much as a second's pause, but the third and oldest member of the trio, Tekaro, hit a large stumbling block as he tried to follow his friends.

Argon snatched hold of the ninja's ankle and brought him to the ground. Still battered and bruised from his flight down the pass, the Gaul was nevertheless seething with rage. His face had become a messy network of cuts and scratches, and his arms and legs throbbed with pain, but he wriggled on to his feet and snatched hold of the fallen assassin with all his strength, hauling the little warrior to his feet. Dazed as he was, however, his punches flew wide of the mark, and Argon soon found himself madly clinging to a scrap of clothing as the ninja expertly twisted and slithered from his grasp.

'Olu!' Argon screamed up at the high pass. 'Help me, here! This one is ... too ... fast.'

There was no reply from above; Olu still lay motionless on the ground, and Argon's voice simply echoed in the empty landscape.

Having broken free of the Gaul's powerful grip, the ninja was now using Argon's own strength against him. He ducked under the muscular arms and employed the momentum of each blow to help him unbalance the Gaul at every turn. In no time at all, the strategy worked. Argon slipped and crashed back on to the path, this time rolling right on to the rocks beside the lagoon.

The ninja wasted no time. Snaking a hand down to his side, he drew a blade so well concealed that it appeared, at first, to be an extension of his own arm. Black-handled and needle-thin, it was obviously a weapon of death-dealing ferocity.

Above the foray, Olu regained consciousness. The former slave shook his head to dislodge the wave of pain in his throat, but immediately remembered how he'd got it and hurriedly struggled to his feet.

Staggering a few paces down the path, he quickly saw Argon. The big Gaul was lying face down on the rocks beside the lagoon, scrambling for a handhold as he tried to raise himself on to his knees.

Behind him, one of the black-clad attackers

had drawn a blade and was advancing fast . . . too fast.

Argon was dead.

Olu realized with an instant, agonizing terror that he was too far away to help. Even if he took a long run up and leapt with every last reserve of his dexterity, he could never hope to reach the side of his fallen friend. He could only watch, a knot in his stomach, as the little ninja raised the sword above his head . . . and brought it down in a sharp stabbing motion.

The blade whistled through the air, sunlight glinting on its surface.

Olu closed his eyes, and felt the tears well up inside him. He took a deep, deep breath and counted to three.

One . . .

Two ...

Three ...

When he reopened his eyes, an extraordinary scene greeted him.

Argon was still wriggling over the jagged rocks, the deadly blade was wedged in a nearby tree and the murderous ninja himself was staggering backwards and forwards between the trees, shaking his head.

Ruma had exploded from the lagoon, landing a punch, which had evidently knocked the little warrior sideways. Now the scrawny Etrurian was slowly stalking his opponent ... and he looked determined to finish the fight, once and for all.

Olu breathed a tearful sigh of relief, and thanked the gods for Ruma's timely return.

He began to hurry down the path towards the combat.

But before he reached the clearing, something completely unexpected happened . . .

CHAPTER II

THE SKY PILLARS

Gladius stopped running and collapsed on to his knees, his breath coming in fits and bursts. He knew for a fact that at least one of the ninjas had pursued him; a brief glance over his shoulder on the edge of the pass had told him that. He also knew that every second he rested took valuable distance from his fast shrinking lead. His vision still blurred from the exhausting run, he took one final gulp of air, stood up and fought his way onward once again.

The trees were thinning out now, and Gladius put on an extra burst of speed to clear the last few clusters so that he could gather a better idea of the vast land beyond.

Stopping beside a large boulder that might, he hoped, screen him from view at the edge of the treeline, Gladius raised a hand to his forehead and squinted all around him.

It seemed he had two very stark choices: to the north lay a range of low hills, mostly rocky and bare of foliage; to the south a series of flat, empty fields seemed to stretch out as far as the eye could see.

Weighing up his choices, Gladius quickly ruled out the high path. He would be easy to see on the hills until he'd crested the first few, and that could take him far too long.

He made up his mind, and headed for the low lands, moving at a steady speed instead of a sprint: he no longer had the energy for anything more.

A few minutes after Gladius had disappeared from view, the ninja Miriki emerged from the trees at a determined run. Glancing in both directions, he studied the landscape with slow and careful precision, watching first the hills and then the distant fields for any detectable sign of movement.

At length, he began to stride towards the first hill, his legs working faster and faster as he picked up the pace. Familiar with the sort of endurance required to fight several opponents at once, Miriki conquered the hill in just a few minutes, needing barely a second more to pause for breath at the top. Then, turning on his feet, he reached down to a strap beside his tightly-clad shin, and produced a small looking-tube from within.

Bringing the object to his eye, he stared down at the fields below the range and, shifting so slightly that he appeared not to move at all, began to study each one in depth. The looking-tube showed patches and patches of blank, empty land . . . and just a single speck, still moving steadily, in one of the furthest fields.

Miriki removed his mask and allowed himself a smile. The fool was overweight and exhausted; he would be no match at all.

Replacing the black cloth that covered his head, the ninja took a moment to check his weapons. Then he began to walk, at a leisurely stroll, in pursuit of his intended victim.

Gladius ventured beyond the last field and found himself half running, half stumbling down the side of a wide valley of grasslands beyond. A quick glance up would have told him he was in a very strange place indeed, but he could not afford such luxuries, and so soldiered on until he almost ran into the first pillar.

Gladius rested against the stone for a few seconds, allowed himself three deep breaths and then took several steps back in order to see where he was.

He almost fell over.

The pillar had to be more than thirty metres tall, and appeared to be made of carved stone. It was cold to the touch, not much wider than two or three hand-spans across and was covered in small handholds and niches that looked to be carved directly into the surface.

Gladius craned his neck to peer up at the top

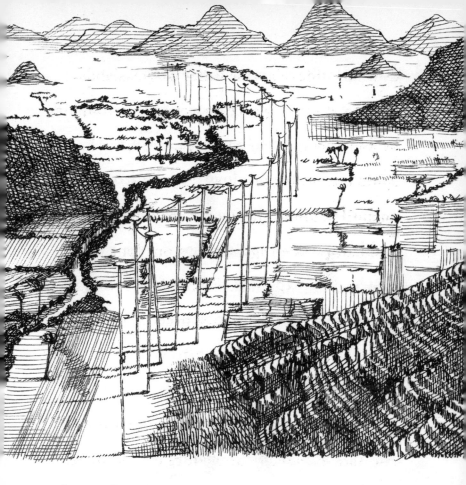

of the pillar, and was surprised to see a platform.

It was perfectly circular, seemed to be made of

wood and certainly not big enough to stand on

for any decent length of time. His eyes followed

a rope attached to the platform and he found

himself looking at a similar pillar a short distance away. Stepping aside, Gladius thought he could make out a line of the curious structures stretching along the length of the valley. They were all attached via ropes, and he could see no discernible reason for their existence. Perhaps they were used in some sort of endurance exercise, like the ones Doom used in his sadistic games back at Arena Primus.

Gladius shook himself from his thoughts, and was about to run on when a sudden impulse overtook him. Before he could give the matter due consideration, he found himself climbing the strange pillar, digging his fingers and toes into each and every niche as he went. He imagined that he looked, from the ground, like a rather large and elderly spider climbing with painful slowness up an impossibly long strand of thread.

The air began to whistle around Gladius as he reached the halfway point, determined not to look down as a mixture of dizziness and nausea overcame him. The only thing spurring him on was the thought that, somewhere close on his trail, the deadly ninja was undoubtedly still coming for him.

The rest of the climb was long and arduous. He didn't know for sure how much time it had taken him to reach the platform, but it certainly felt as though an hour had passed . . . maybe two.

In fact, it had taken Gladius a little under twenty minutes to reach the top of the pillar. His fingers found the platform before he actually looked up and saw it.

His first feeling was one of relief: the platform was slightly bigger than it had first appeared from the ground.

Gladius gripped the edge of the wood and hauled himself on to the surface of the platform. His arms and legs dangled pathetically over the sides, but he could at least breathe a little while the majority of his bulk was supported.

It was then that he saw the ninja arrive on the edge of the valley.

Walking with an almost casual swing to his step, the black-clad warrior paused briefly to survey the landscape before moving on down the side of the valley.

Great, Gladius thought. Of all the stupid ideas I've ever had, this one takes some beating. I've made myself completely visible up here . . .

you can probably see me from half a mile away. Apart from anything else, I'm completely trapped and totally isolated. Fantastic – what else can go wrong?

As if in answer to the question, there was a sudden, terrifying creak and the entire pillar shifted beneath him.

Gladius cried out with shock, and clamped on to the platform like a limpet taking hold of a pebble.

It isn't stable, he thought, his mind racing with fear. Those ropes aren't just connecting the pillars – they're holding them upright! Argghhh!

Keeping as still as possible, Gladius felt sweat begin to bead on his brow. Casting a glance at the ground, he cursed again: the ninja was heading directly for the base of the pillar.

As danger gathered all around him, Gladius tried to think of Decimus and what his fiery friend would do in such a grim situation. Then he began, very slowly, to move.

Gripping the platform tightly with both hands, he lifted himself on to his knees. The pillar trembled slightly, and rocked almost imperceptibly as his arms trembled. Puffing out a breath of air that cooled the sweat glistening on his lips, he quickly lifted one leg and put a foot flat to the platform. Again, it shifted slightly as the rope securing it to the neighbouring pillar was pulled taut, and once more it held fast.

Knowing the most difficult manoeuvre was still ahead of him, Gladius swallowed and then simply performed the stunt without thinking first. Bringing the other leg forward with surprising speed, he lifted himself on to his feet and threw both arms outward in an effort to steady his balance.

For a few, mind-numbing seconds he simply stood atop the shaking pillar with his legs trembling beneath him and his arms moving frantically either side of him. At first it looked as though he would bring the entire pillar crashing to the ground, killing himself in the process, but the rope won out and the pillar – despite its sudden shift – held firm.

Gladius waited for his balance to even out, tensing every muscle against the onrush of air. His eyes streaming with tears, he prayed to every god he'd ever heard of to spare him the great fall.

Then Gladius did something he knew was completely insane: he looked down.

Unbelievable! The ninja was climbing up the pillar towards him. Moving with customary speed, he was already closing on Gladius when the big youth realized how crazy the chase was. If the ninja continued to climb, the pillar would be totally top-heavy, and they'd both end up . . .

Suddenly, a powerful surge of inspiration flashed through his mind.

Come on then, great warrior,

he thought. Come and slaughter the

boy on the spike: no problem for an expert

killer like you . . .

Gladius waited until the ninja was

approximately three quarters of the way up the

pillar. Then he swung both arms out behind

him, and leapt on to the rope.

For a split second he sailed through the air,

his mind maddened with the horror of exactly

what it was that he was doing.

Below, the ninja froze like an alley cat,

suddenly aware that something unexpected had

happened.

Gladius dived on to the rope, catching it with

arms and legs hooked so that he immediately swung to the underside of it. Moving as though he were practically weightless, the big youth scrambled along the rope, assisted by the fact that the pillar was falling towards him. The momentum all on his side, Gladius found himself gliding downward, faster and faster.

Suddenly, the rope jarred to a halt.

Gladius craned his neck around to see what was happening above him.

The pillar had stopped moving, presumably as a result of some prop or barrier in the ground at its base. Now it stood at a sharp angle with the field far below it, and the ninja dangled helplessly from the handhold. His grip was evidently weakening, as Gladius saw that his kicks were becoming more and more frantic as he tried in vain to swing himself around. A single foot in one of the carved niches would have seen the little warrior saved, but he was hanging too vertically to get a foothold on the pillar.

Sensing the advantage, Gladius lost all sense of fear and began to bounce, drag and thrash himself around on the rope, employing both his weight and his strength to cause as much pull on the line as possible.

It worked. The pillar jarred once again, barely moving more than a few inches, but it was enough to dislodge the precarious assassin.

With a cry born of panic and horror, the little ninja plummeted to the ground, tumbling head over feet until he hit the grass with a soft, wet thud.

At first, peering down at the field, Gladius suspected that the fall had killed him. Then he saw the black-clad figure reach an arm around to grasp the back of his head. A leg twitched; once, twice.

The assassin clambered untidily to his feet, made to move a few steps and collapsed again. He rolled around once more, a few seconds later, but with incredible difficulty. If Gladius was going to save himself from this terrible situation, he needed to do something right now.

Gathering the energy he had in his last reserves, Gladius continued along the rope, counting under his breath in order to take his mind off the agonizing pain coursing through his arms and legs.

His progression to the next pillar was far

more difficult, as the momentum was against him and he was effectively climbing the rope as if it hung down from an impossibly high ceiling.

Just when he thought his arms might actually fall off, he made the second platform and scrambled on to it, rolling over like a beached whale in order take in great lungfuls of the cold air that rushed past.

No time to lie around up here, though. Got to move; got to move now.

Gladius crawled over the edge of the platform and lowered himself on to the first sets of footholds. Then he began to climb down the pillar, his confidence increasing as he drew closer and closer to the ground.

The ninja wasn't on the patch of field where he'd landed, but he wasn't too far away, either.

Gladius squinted into the afternoon sun and held up a hand to shield his eyes as he saw the little warrior sliding across the grass a short distance away. Moving like a tortoise with two broken legs or a squirming, wounded snake, the ninja was trying and failing to get to his feet.

Gladius tightened his jaw and marched after the little warrior. Seeing his abandoned sword in the ground, he snatched it up, testing its weight as he went. When he neared the prone figure, he crouched to clap a firm hold on the ninja's ankle and dragged him around in the grass. Then, screaming a battle cry of his own, Gladius began to pound across the field, dragging the little warrior behind him. Moving on up the valley and leaving the grasslands behind him, he hauled the ninja over rocks, through scrub bushes, along dusty paths and over rugged ground.

Miriki, half-dazed and badly wounded, mumbled a series of fractured sentences and some unrecognizable pleas before Gladius dumped him, unceremoniously, beside a rotted tree.

Gladius moved to stand in front of his opponent and quickly levelled the assassin's own sword at him. Then he ripped off the mask that covered most of the man's face, and stood back.

'You're not much older than me!' he said, with unconcealed surprise. 'Hmm . . . I can't tell if you're the one who beat me at the Winter Palace

or not, but it doesn't really matter. If it was you

standing here with this sword, I don't doubt you

would already have killed me . . . but I'm not

like that.' He leaned down, put the sword blade

under Miriki's bloodied chin, and smiled. 'I

don't suppose you can understand me very well,'

he muttered. 'But that doesn't matter, either. I'm

not going to kill you, because I'm not a killer . . .

but since I can't have you following me, I need to make sure you . . . stay put.'

He swung the sword pommel around, knocking the ninja out, cold. Then he began to remove the little warrior's clothes, finding several curious weapons in the process. There were three metal discs, a silvery star with sharp edges and two more daggers hidden in his garb. Pocketing these, Gladius tore the black cloth into several strips and used them to secure the ninja to the tree.

This done, he crested the high end of the valley, and looked to the patchwork of fields beyond.

Decimus had said he would come and find him after dealing with the other assassin . . . but what if he couldn't? What if the assassin dispatched him? Moreover, what if Olu and Argon were still at the mercy of the third warrior, even now begging for their lives?

Gladius looked toward the horizon, and realized that he faced a grim choice.

CHAPTER III

RED MIST

The ninja Tekaro was more deadly than either of his companions, and not simply because he was the oldest of the three and their appointed leader. In truth, Aritezu was the most cunning fighter, and Miriki couldn't be matched for speed, but both ninjas had their weaknesses. Aritezu could be overconfident, while Miriki sometimes displayed a stupidity that made one wonder how he had ever been granted admission to the order. Tekaro, however . . . was different.

A fiery and aggressive combatant, the senior ninja was also creative in other ways . . . like his innate ability with herbal compounds. While Aritezu and Miriki were in the fields, exercising or engaging each other in training duels, Tekaro spent his time inventing and researching some truly ingenious poisons. He called these his 'last resorts' and reserved them for times when he truly felt himself to be in dire peril.

For Tekaro, such a time had come. The surprise attack from the boy who had been hiding in the lagoon had knocked the wind out of him, and he didn't have the energy to fight this ambush and the two others now advancing on him.

No . . . desperate times called for desperate measures.

Tekaro spun around and flung out his arm.

The cloud of dust exploded in the clearing, a red mist that hit Ruma full in the face, engulfing his head entirely for a second. The scrawny Etrurian had no chance to defend himself or cover his eyes, and the effects were severe.

Apart from a stinging sensation in his eyes upon impact, he'd also taken in a considerable amount of the powder through his nose and mouth. Almost immediately, he felt dizzy, unbalanced and disoriented. He made two steps forward and several back before colliding with a tree and collapsing on to the ground. There, he convulsed as if he had been struck by lightning, his screams echoing around the lagoon.

It took Olu, who was still approaching from the higher path, several seconds to realize that the ninja had thrown a handful of dust into the face of his friend. Argon, on the other hand, was in a better position to recognize what had happened.

The Gaul hurled himself across the clearing and cannoned into the ninja, lifting him off his feet and slamming him against a tree trunk.

Still half dazed from Ruma's ambush at the lagoon, Tekaro tried his best to block every punch, but Argon was fighting with a determined ferocity.

When Olu leapt into the fray and clamped
both arms around the ninja's slight frame,
Tekaro knew instinctively that he was finished.

Three more kicks disarmed the warrior totally, and his defences ebbed away with the last of his energy.

Argon swung wide with a bunched fist and drove it hard into the ninja's masked jaw, blasting him into unconsciousness.

As Tekaro crumpled into a heap at their feet, Olu spotted the thin, half-concealed blade at his side and greedily snatched it up.

Argon turned on his heel and prepared to hurry to Ruma's side, but a last-minute glance back at Olu caused him to dive in front of the ninja as his friend raised the weapon to strike.

'Olu! Olu! What are you doing? We can't kill him . . .'

'Why not? He would have killed us! Look what he did to Ruma!'

Argon peered down at the Etrurian, who was still writing on the path, clutching his face and moaning loudly.

'We don't know how badly Ruma is hurt,' he protested. 'Besides, I'm not comfortable killing people in cold blood – we don't even know why they attacked us yet. If we can bring Ruma out of that terrible state he's in, he might even know who they are!'

Olu reluctantly lowered the sword, but he didn't follow Argon to Ruma's side. Instead, he crouched beside the ninja and held the sword away from him, ready to strike at any moment. With his free hand, he removed the mask that covered Tekaro's face and searched the assassin for any other weapons. All he discovered, however, was an empty pouch containing a trace

of the red powder that had been thrown at
Ruma.

Further down the path, Argon had to grip
Ruma by the shoulders and apply great
pressure in order to stop his friend thrashing
around. Even so, Ruma was still shaking
violently, his eyes rolling back in his head.
The powder had mixed with the Etrurian's tears
to form a red liquid that streamed down
his cheeks.

'Ruma! Ruma! It's Argon – can you hear me?'

'Arghghghghgh! Stop them! Stop them! Help me! Help meeee! No! Nooooooooo!'

'Stop who?' the Gaul exclaimed. 'How can I help you, Ruma? Can you hear me at all? How can I help?'

Argon cast a worried glance at Olu, who shook his head in disbelief.

Ruma's face was now a mask of madness. His eyes were pure white, the pupils shrivelled away to pinpoints, and his mouth narrowed into a cold slit.

A dark feeling stole over Argon as he looked upon his friend, and again he attempted to communicate with the Etrurian.

'It's me, Ruma. It's ARGON. I'm going to try something that might seem crazy ... but I don't know how else to save you.'

The words barely out of his lips, Argon suddenly heaved Ruma on to his shoulder and ran down to the side of the lagoon, where he dumped the scrawny Etrurian in the fresh waters and promptly dived in after him.

Olu turned to the ninja who still lay propped against the tree, and slapped him hard in the face.

'Wake up, you cursed wretch!' he spat. 'What have you done to our friend? I said WAKE UP.' A second slap failed to wake the warrior, so Olu simply pushed him on to his side and hurried to the base of the lagoon to help Argon with Ruma.

As he reached the bank, however, the big Gaul was already emerging from the pool, hauling the Etrurian after him.

'You really think that was a good idea?' Olu enquired. 'Dropping him in the lagoon and half drowning him?'

Argon shrugged. 'I hoped it would shock him awake, but look – he's not coughing water or anything.'

They both looked down at Ruma.

The Etrurian had stopped shaking, but now he seemed to be in a deep, disturbed sleep. His chest was rising and falling rhythmically, while his eyelids pulsed and trembled as if the eyes beneath them were still darting left and right.

'I'm worried,' Argon admitted. 'I'm really, really worried. Where in the seven hells is Decimus when you need him?' He quickly held up his hands as Olu began to protest. 'I know, I know – he distracted those other two and probably saved us, but we could really do with his help, here.'

'We should take him back to the boat,' Olu pointed out. 'Maybe Tonino will be able to help him?'

Argon shook his head. 'We came to find all of them, Olu. We can't just turn around and head back without Decimus and Gladius. If we wait here for a while, they might come back this way. They know we're here, now, after all.'

'Yeah,' said Olu, doubtfully. 'But what if those warriors kill them both and it's them that come back this way? It took three of us to take out one of these lunatics. How are we going to cope against two?'

'I still say we wait,' Argon snapped. 'If the enemy arrives first, then so be it. I can't even work out why they are the enemy – they just attacked us without giving us a chance to communicate with them.'

Olu returned his attention to the unconscious ninja, and whistled between his teeth.

'At least we have this one's weapons,' he muttered. 'Including a little of that dust he used on Ruma. Only the gods know what it's done to his mind . . .'

They both looked down at Ruma, who had begun to stir in his sleep.

CHAPTER IV

DEATH IN THE DARKNESS

The ninja Aritezu had pursued Decimus Rex into the hills beyond the pass. He was also a stranger to Yelang, having only been in the king's service for a short time, but he had spared no effort to find his intended victim. Always one to outshine his brothers in both determination and guile, Aritezu was undoubtedly the most educated of the group; he could speak and understand several languages, work out strategies for advanced combat and even track an opponent by the disturbance of dust on the ground. In short, Aritezu was a formidable warrior. He put on an incredible burst of speed, catching sight of the Roman shortly after they had left the tree line. Now, some time later, he had the boy firmly in his sights. When he finally topped the ridge they had both been climbing, however, he was somewhat surprised to come across an open cave.

Aritezu peered around him. There was nowhere else for the Roman to run; he would have been visible had he fled down the rise in either direction. There was only the cave.

Aritezu laughed: exactly how stupid was this fool?

His answer came in the form of a shouted challenge, which echoed around the mouth of the cave. It was definitely coming from within.

'I'm hiding in the darkness,' said the voice. 'I doubt you understand the language I speak, but you should be able to find me if you follow my voice.'

The words took several seconds to die away; the cave had to be deep.

Aritezu smiled humourlessly.

'I understand your language perfectly, boy,' he called back. 'But I confess that I do not understand your stupidity.'

The ninja strode toward the mouth of the cave, his footsteps almost silent as he studied the ground before him. The tracks were clear and easy to follow.

'You understand me well!' cried the voice, once again. 'And you speak my own language better than I do, it seems. To that end, hear now my words: I am Decimus Rex, Destroyer of Arenas, Defeater of Traps, Evader of Death and Commander of Combat. You would be wise to walk away from my voice ... and not towards it.'

Aritezu merely smiled, and continued into the cave. At the first junction, he listened carefully to the echo that died away as Decimus finished speaking. Then, almost mechanically, he turned left and walked down a sloping path into the gloom. Darkness held no fear for Aritezu; he was trained to fight in all conditions, and had tackled several of his past opponents in the pitch dark, his eyes restricted by a folding cloth.

'Keep talking, Great Decimus,' he yelled, suddenly crouching and drawing his sword. 'I am Aritezu, and everything you need to know about me you will quickly discover upon our next meeting.' He smiled in the darkness. 'If, that is, you and your pathetic friends didn't suffer enough of a beating on our first encounter at the Winter Palace. I can still taste your blood, in fact . . . '

The voice rang out again; it was much closer this time.

'Good . . . in a few seconds, you will be able to compare it with the taste of your own.'

Aritezu crawled on his hands and knees along a new tunnel to his left, his thin sword now clamped firmly between his teeth.

Just a little further . . .

Despite the darkness, he could feel Decimus creeping through the shadows ahead of him. Slowly and very deliberately, he removed the sword from his mouth and leapt forward.

Decimus prided himself on his ability to outguess a good opponent. It was his use of this skill that had worked so well for him, both during his time at Arena Primus and afterwards. Now, however, he found himself matched in every respect.

When the assassin emerged from the shadows, he did so with such lightning haste that Decimus barely had time to turn and raise his arms before he was swept off his feet.

Within seconds, he was struggling beneath the crazed ninja, desperately trying to stay the blade that was being driven towards his neck.

'Argghhhhh!'

Decimus gritted his teeth and called upon every ounce of energy he had at his command, and screamed with rage as he wrestled with Aritezu. Unfortunately, the ninja had both the advantage and the momentum.

Snarling with the effort of his own frantic determination, Aritezu forced the blade downward. As he felt the edge draw even closer to the scarred flesh of Decimus's neck, his snarls turned to cruel cackles of delight.

Twisting beneath the frenzied assault, the young gladiator finally dropped his guard, but before the blade met skin, he swiftly brought up a knee with all his might.

Aritezu wore no armour; his basic training

promoted the use of stealth over strength, and armour was simply counterproductive when sneaking up on an opponent.

Swords could be dodged, daggers deflected, obstacles vaulted over. The knee of Decimus Rex, however, presented an unexpected development.

It also found its mark.

Aritezu gasped with the dull shock of the pain that was suddenly coursing through his groin. His eyes welling up with tears, the ninja dropped his sword and heard it clatter to the ground as he collapsed sideways.

Aritezu quickly discovered that his mask had become a hazard. The pain was such that the heat from his tears was plastering the cloth to his face. He reached up a hand and ripped it off.

Decimus had scrambled on to his feet in the darkness and was even now feeling around for the sword, his rough hands working quickly over the cold stone floor of the passage.

Aritezu knew he had to retreat, if only for the few seconds it would take him to recover from the blow. Using his superior sense of awareness in the dark, he rolled over backwards and slunk away down a side corridor. There, still breathing heavily from the pain, he reached into the concealed pockets on his other leg in order to produce three metal stars with razor-sharp edges. If he couldn't defeat this wretch in hand-to-hand combat, he would simply kill him at a distance.

He'd barely given the thought time to develop when the disgustingly triumphant voice struck up again in the darkness.

'How is the taste of my blood when mixed with your own tears, Aritezu?'

The ninja swore under his breath, and pulled himself to his feet. Slowly, carefully, he crept towards the dying echo.

'I have your sword,' Decimus continued. 'If you come out of the shadows now and surrender, I give you my word that you will come to no further harm. You are but a servant of Slavious Doom . . . you are not Doom himself.'

Aritezu took a new route this time, diverting his path down several new passages until he could feel himself approaching the young gladiator at a new angle. The ranged attack would not be expected, and certainly wouldn't be defended.

He pitched back an arm, and let the first star fly. It whistled through the air, and then . . . nothing.

Aritezu squinted into the darkness. There was no unwelcome clatter of the star glancing off the rock wall, but no welcome thud of Decimus crashing to the floor, either.

The ninja waited, and was astonished to hear the voice resound once again.

'Your last chance, Aritezu. Lay down your arms and surrender to me. You will be spared.'

Impossible – it was as if the shadows had swallowed the star before it even reached its target.

Aritezu leapt across the passage and hurled a second missile . . . but, again, no noise accompanied its flight.

A second passed in silence, then another . . . and, finally, the voice echoed through the caves yet again.

'Throw one more star, ninja, and I will not simply block it with my sword as I have done with the two before – I swear I will kill you where you stand.'

Inconceivable – this Roman idiot was capable of blocking shuriken stars thrown by an expert marksman in the pitch dark? Surely the heathen gods must be watching over him! Well, his luck couldn't last for ever.

Aritezu allowed himself a sly smile, and stepped into the very centre of the passage. He threw the final star with such force that the effort propelled his entire body forward.

Again, the silence endured. This time, however, the lack of noise was quickly disturbed by the whirring of a spinning blade that whistled through the air and hit its target squarely in the chest.

Aritezu staggered backwards, one hand weakly probing for the blade sticking out of his chest. His vision swam as the shock hit every part of his body; he collided with several walls before dropping on to his knees and folding over.

The ninja stared into the black abyss and spat a few, last, desperate words:

'Your . . . gods . . . protected . . . y—'

Then he collapsed on to the floor of the tunnel, and he didn't move again.

Several minutes later, Decimus Rex emerged from the cave mouth and blinked at the waning light of the afternoon sun. Despite the late hour, he could feel the warmth of the rays washing over his face in a way that made him realize he had never truly appreciated the sun before.

Decimus Rex smiled at the heavens. Then he looked down at his ravaged body.

Three stars, three wounds: each, on their own, potentially fatal.

Decimus smiled distractedly as he watched the blood seep from his chest, his side, his neck . . .

then the great gladiator fell to the ground and tumbled down the hillside.

At the foot of a plain and unremarkable hill on the edge of Yelang, Decimus Rex stared up at the shifting clouds ... and began to die.

CHAPTER
V

DARK

DREAMS

'I hope he's OK,' said Gladius, kneeling beside Ruma as Argon and Olu finished securing the barely conscious Tekaro to the tree. They had agreed upon the idea of using the ninja's garments as bindings when Gladius had related his own encounter with the third warrior.

'At least he's breathing properly, now,' said the Gaul.

Gladius shook his head. 'I'm not talking about Ruma,' he muttered. 'I should never have come back here – you both had the situation under control.' He let out a deep and concerned sigh. 'I should have gone after Decimus, instead; these assassins are really, really dangerous . . . especially one on one.'

Olu patted his friend on the back.

'Relax, Gladius; if you won against one, I'm pretty sure Decimus will be fine.'

The three friends returned their attention to Ruma, and almost sprang back when the scrawny Etrurian's eyelids flicked open.

His thoughts still swimming from the dreams that had almost consumed him entirely,

Ruma looked up, wide-eyed, at the three worried faces hovering over him.

'Are – are you OK?' Olu ventured.

'It's us, Ruma,' added Argon, smiling warmly. 'It's Gladius, Olu and Argon. Can you hear me?'

The Etrurian treated them all to a baleful stare, then began to move his cracked lips.

'I can hear you,' he muttered. 'And, of course, I know who you are. It's who I am that's causing me the problems.'

He let out a weak laugh, and was quickly joined by hysterical laughter from his overjoyed companions.

Gladius didn't waste any more time. He jumped up immediately and headed for the far side of the lagoon.

'I'm going to find Decimus,' he called back,

as Argon helped their tired friend to his feet. 'You three stay here until I get back … and make sure Ruma gets some food. Watch that ninja, too – he's still dangerous.'

As Olu fussed over Ruma, fetching him water and trying to get him to eat some soft cuts of bread, the Etrurian just continued to glance around him as if he was a baby, seeing the world

for the very first time.

Inside his head, though, the dream images still began to swirl. Horrible, tangible nightmares that had revealed the truth to him. Faces blurred, and memories swam together, exchanging places in his mind as the poison worked to confuse him. He'd been snatched from his family, tortured in the trials and dragged halfway across the world to rescue someone who was already dead . . . and all thanks to Decimus Rex.

How could Slavious Doom be a more vile enemy than that whispering wretch, Decimus, in their midst. He was always egging them all on to greater and greater peril in the name of some pathetic quest. Those other fools were just as bad, following him all the time and expecting

Ruma to do the same ... well, not any more ...

Now, Decimus Rex would pay for destroying Ruma's life. He would pay very dearly ...

COMING SOON

As Decimus Rex lies dying in the hills of Yelang, Gladius mounts a desperate search for his friend. Elsewhere, Olu and Argon continue to aid Ruma, completely unaware that the Etrurian's mind is now poisoned against them . . .

Can the group survive long enough to thwart Slavious Doom's evil plans once again? And, if Teo is really alive, can they find him? Find out now in . . .

THE INSANE FURY

GLADIATOR BOY

CAN'T WAIT UNTIL THE NEXT
GLADIATOR BOY COMES OUT?

DESPERATE TO KNOW WHAT
HAPPENS NEXT?

Find out now on
WWW.GLADIATORBOY.COM
with an exclusive online story from
David Grimstone!

GLADIATOR GAME
DEADLY BATTLES

Randomly determine who goes first.

The first player secretly chooses a weak spot and writes that down (example: Chin is no. 2). They then note down the numbers of any three places that they will always defend against automatically. The rest of the locations are undefended.

The second player does the same.

Playing in turn, each player announces a place where he will strike his opponent. If he strikes in the weak spot, his opponent is defeated immediately. If he strikes in an undefended location, 1 point (or wound) is scored. If he strikes in a defended location, no points are scored. Each location may only be struck once per game.

The first player to take 4 wounds is defeated!

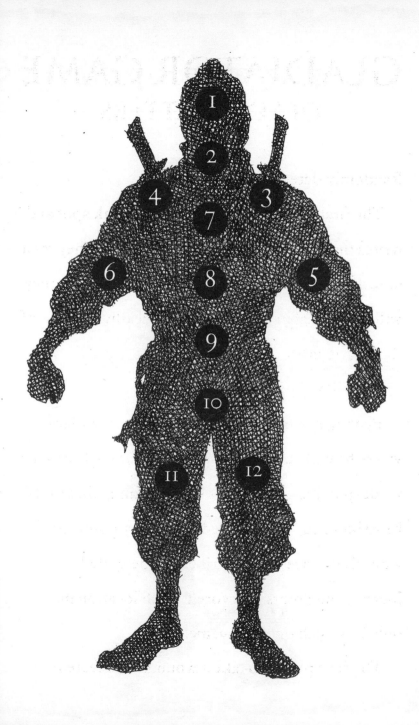

CHARACTER PROFILES

THE THREE NINJAS

NAME: Miriki, Aritezu, Tekaro

FROM: Plains of Iga, Japan

HEIGHT: 1.68 metres, 1.73 metres and 1.70 metres

BODY TYPE: Lean, slight (all)

COMBAT SIGNAL:

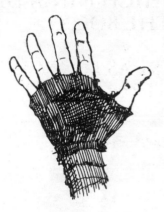

Open Hand (Miriki)

Closed Fist (Aritezu)

Crossed Fists (Tekaro)

NINJA QUIZ: How well do you know the three ninjas? Can you answer the following questions?

1. WHICH OF THE NINJAS PURSUES GLADIUS WHEN THE TRIO SPLIT UP TO FOLLOW THE SLAVES?

2. WHICH NINJA DIES AT THE END OF THE BOOK?

3. LIST AS MANY AS YOU CAN OF ARITEZU'S SPECIAL SKILLS.

Fact File:
* The ninjas are Japanese, not Chinese.
* The eldest is Tekaro.
* The youngest is Miriki.

Answers: 1. Miriki. P.41 2. Aritezu, P.92 3. Various – see: p.78, p.81.

GLADIATOR BOY

WWW.GLADIATORBOY.COM

Have you checked out the Gladiator Boy website?
It's the place to go for games, downloads,
activities, sneak previews and lots of fun!

Sign up to the newsletter at
WWW.GLADIATORBOY.COM
and receive exclusive extra
content and the opportunity
to enter special members-only
competitions.